This book belongs to:

Rose

romantically ridiculous animal rhymes

Margaret K. McElderry Books
New York London Toronto Sydney

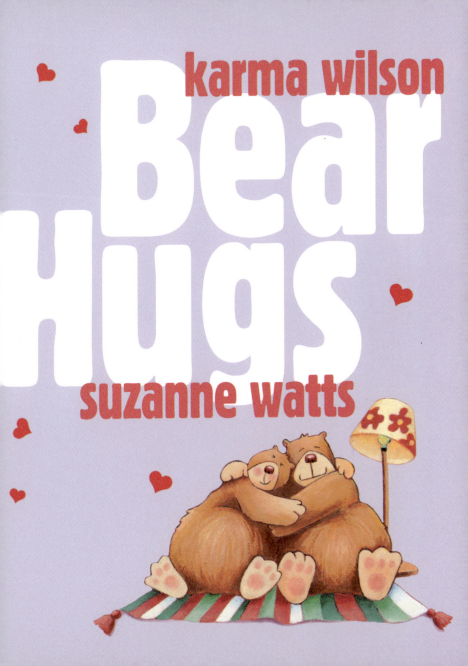

MARGARET K. McELDERRY BOOKS
An imprint of Simon & Schuster Children's Publishing Division
1230 Avenue of the Americas, New York, New York 10020
Text copyright © 2005 by Karma Wilson
Illustrations copyright © 2005 by Suzanne Watts
This edition, 2009
MARGARET K. McELDERRY BOOKS is a trademark of Simon & Schuster, Inc.
For information about special discounts for bulk purchases,
please contact Simon & Schuster Special Sales at 1-866-506-1949
or business@simonandschuster.com.
The Simon & Schuster Speakers Bureau can bring authors to your live event.
For more information or to book an event,
contact the Simon & Schuster Speakers Bureau at 1-866-248-3049
or visit our website at www.simonspeakers.com.
Book design by Lauren Rille
The text for this book is set in Lomba.
The illustrations for this book are rendered in alkyd oil paint.
Manufactured in China
First Edition
10 9 8 7 6 5 4 3 2 1
Library of Congress Cataloging-in-Publication Data
Wilson, Karma.
Bear hugs : romantically ridiculous animal rhymes / Karma Wilson ;
illustrated by Suzanne Watts.—1st ed.
p. cm.
Summary: A collection of eighteen short poems celebrating love and friendship
between animals, from cats and sheep to giraffes and crocodiles.
ISBN: 978-0-689-85763-8 (hc)
1. Animals—Juvenile poetry. 2. Children's poetry, American. [1. Animals—Poetry.
2. Love—Poetry. 3. American poetry.] I. Watts, Suzanne, ill. II. Title.
PS3623.I5854R47 2005   811'.6—dc21   2003007914
ISBN: 978-1-4169-9427-5 (paper-over-board)

To my husband, Scott—
who puts up with my morning-breath "rhinocerkisses"
and gives great "bear hugs."

—k. w.

For Mum and Dad

—s. w.

Table of Contents

Rhinocerkiss

Rhino Mister and Rhino Miss
gaze at the moon in rhino bliss.
They rub their rhino tusks like this.
And now you've seen
rhinocerkiss!

Pocket FULL of Posies

A kangaroo hopped happily,
her pocket full of posies.
She gave her bouquet to a kanga-gent,
who blushed from head to toes-ies.

Turtle Love

He finally came out of his shell
and asked if she'd go on a date.
It only took them five hours or so
to clean off their dinner plate.
They went for a stroll in the moonlight.
He said, "You're my turtle dove."
She said, "And you're my man of steel."
Now *that* is turtle love.

17

Bear Hugs

When this burly pair hugs,
it's tender-loving-care hugs,
twirling-in-the-air hugs,
cuddled-in-the-lair hugs,
here-and-everywhere hugs!
They sure like to share hugs.
Aww, of course . . .
it's bear hugs!

The Cat's Meow

I'll cuddle and purr.
I'll groom my soft fur,
all for my favorite guy.
I can't help but boast
of the one I love most—
Me, Myself, and I.

Always Remember

"Remember me forever," he said.
"Remember the love that we shared.
Remember the way we danced trunk to trunk.
Remember how much that I cared.
Always remember our time spent together
from the first day that we met!"
"I will," she replied. "Don't you remember?
Elephants never forget!"

Pignic

The basket is packed
with goodies to eat.
The two wallow down in the shade.
They gaze at each other with love in their eye
and sip at their sweet lemonade.
"I adore you, my dear."
"I adore you as well."
They begin their meal as a pair.
But . . .

Those hogs just don't know how to share!

I'm APE
for You

Eee... Eee...
Eee...

Ooo... Ooo...
Ooo...

It's true, it's true.
I'm ape for you!

Ooo... Ooo...
Ooo...

Eee... Eee... Eee...

I hope that you
are ape for me!

Don't keep me hangin'
in the air.
I have a tree
that we can share.
I'll go bananas
if you don't care.

Ooo...

Ooo...

Ooo...

you do?

A Croak-in' Heart

If you like me,
I'll leap for sheer joy!
If you don't,
my heart will be broke.
If you love me,
I'll croak with delight.
If you don't—
I'll simply croak.

Some Bunny Special

You're sweet as honey,

you beautiful bunny.

You're lovely and gentle and fair.

Your hop is the tops.

You're queen of the lops.

But I'm just an ugly ol' hare.

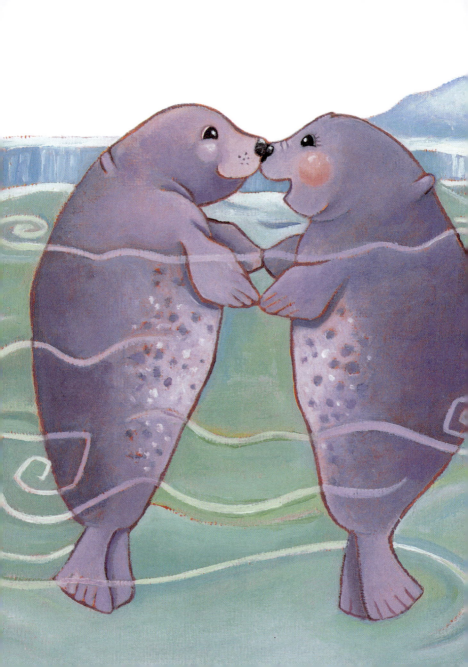

Seal with a KISS

It's signed, sealed, and delivered.
You've made a splash with me.
I just flip when I see your face,
and I hope that you agree.
Let's pledge our love forever.
We'll make it final like this . . .
look in my eyes and I'll look in yours.
MWAA!
Seal with a kiss!

Gimme a Sssqueeeze

If I only had them,
I'd fall on my knee*sss*
and beg you for hour*sss* to
gimme a *sssqueeeeze.*

I'd trade in my *ssskin*
and freeze in the breeze
if it would per*sss*suade you to
gimme a *sssqueeeeze.*

Whoa, you boa,
don't be such a teassse.
Let's sssit ssside by ssside.
Gimme a sssqueeeeze.

You will? Er . . . um . . .
      ssstop!
I . . . can't . . . breathe. . . .
      Wheeze!

What a CHICKEN

Rooster clucks and Rooster struts.

He feels like he could shout.

The sweetest hen, whose name is Gwen,

is something to crow about.

The way she preens till her feathers gleam

makes Rooster stick out his chest.

Just one look is all it took.

He hopes to build her a nest.

But when she's near, an embarrassing fear

makes talking a terrible task.

It seems at this rate he won't get a date.

Rooster's too chicken to ask!

A Moosetake

His antlers gleamed,
but she, it seemed,
was not at all impressed.
He brushed his fur,
but still, to her
he didn't look his best.
He begged and whined,
but she declined.
It wouldn't have worked anyhow.

That crazy moose,
the silly goose,

fell
in
love
with a
Jersey
cow!

Lovebirds

She waddles the isle
in high penguin style,
holding a snow-white bouquet.
Her ivory dress
cost thousands, no less . . .
or that's what the sea lions say.
The sweet maid of honor
has silk draped upon her,
which must have cost dearly as well.
Ice sculptures so steep
do not come too cheap . . .
or that's what the walruses tell.

An orchestra, too?

Amazing but true!

The whales say they charge quite a fee.

The groom looks just smashing—

so dapper, so dashing.

And think . . . his tuxedo was free!

The night was delightful—
  the dancing divine.
Each animal twirled
  with their own valentine.
She sat at the wall
  and swayed to the beat.
She watched and she waited
  and stared at her feet.
But nobody asked her.
  Nobody would.
Well, to be fair,
  nobody could.
Her beauty was stunning.
  But still it was clear:
Something about her
  was hard to get near.

Pins and Needles

She was on pins and needles,
  filled with despair.
And then he swooped in
  with a debonair flair.
She hoped he would ask her,
  but most would decline
to dance cheek to cheek
  with a she-porcupine.
But he was no coward!
  It just took one glance.
"You've pricked at my heart,"
  he said. "Can we dance?"
To him that dear girl
  felt as soft as a pillow.
The prince of her dreams
  was a young armadillo.

Will Ewe?

Will ewe?
Would ewe?
Can ewe?
Could ewe . . .
be my valentine?

Might ewe?
Won't ewe?
Oh, please,
don't ewe . . .
want a ram so fine?

Ewe, my dear,
are sheer delight.
Don't be sheepish.
I don't bite!
I'm not ba-a-ad
and you're just right.

Will ewe please be mine?

Crocodile Tears

A crocodile known as Al
asked a pretty croco-gal
if he might not take her out.
But she turned up her toothsome snout.
She said no, she would not go,
and so . . .
He sniffed and snuffled,
cried and moaned.

He wailed and sobbed.
He bawled and groaned!
He threw a tantrum for a week.
Tears slipped down his bumpy cheek.
He cried for months. He cried for years . . .
giant crocodile tears.
And from that one sad crocodile
flowed the mighty River Nile.

Love-a-bull

Your legs are short and slightly bowed.
You're looking somewhat pigeon-toed.
Your belly almost skims the rug.
Your nose, it shows a bit of pug.
You're not fat, just sort of stout.
When it's hot, your tongue lolls out.
You drool a bit (okay, a lot).
Those are quite some teeth you've got.
It's no bull we're just alike.
So will you, Lola, take me, Spike,
to be your dog eternally?
You see, you're love-a-bull to me.

People Are Animals Too

It's plain as can be,
   so easy to see,
that animals love
   just like you and like me.
And so it seems
   the old saying is true . . .
people are animals too.

We joke with each other,
    like crazy baboons
and laugh together
    like silly old loons.
We hug each other
    like two chimpanzees
and chatter together
    like birds in the trees.
Sometimes we fight
    like a cat and a dog,
but when we make up,
    we're high on the hog.

Like lions we always
   protect those we love.
But in the end,
   when push comes to shove,
we'll stick through
   the hard times together
and rally like birds of a feather.
Yes, people are animals too . . .
and the best kind of
   animal-person is
       YOU!

If you love **Bear Hugs**, collect more books
by Karma Wilson for your very own:

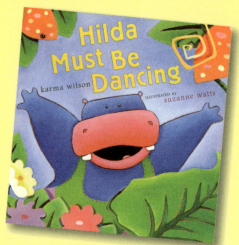

Hilda Must Be Dancing
illustrated by Suzanne Watts

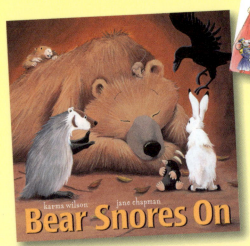

Princess Me
illustrated by Christa Unzner

Bear Snores On
illustrated by Jane Chapm

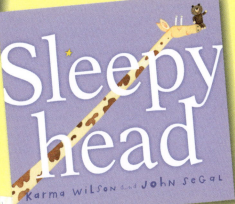

Where Is Home, Little Pip?
illustrated by Jane Chapman

Sleepyhead
illustrated by John Segal

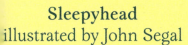

A Frog in the Bog
illustrated by Joan Rankin